P9-CRB-952

For my daughters, Isa, Holly, and Taryn, who are the inspiration for my story
—M. B.

For my mother and father
—D. J.

Hyperion Books for Children, 114 Fifth Avenue, New York, New York 10011-5690.
Printed in the United States of America.

First Edition

1 3 5 7 9 10 8 6 4 2

This book is set in 15-point Centaur.
Designed by Mara Van Fleet.

Library of Congress Cataloging-in-Publication Data
Bolton, Michael.
The secret of the Lost Kingdom / Michael Bolton ; illustrated by
David Jermann. — 1st ed.
p. cm.
Summary: While on a field trip to a grand castle, two classmates meet a mysterious old man who tells them about the treachery and glory surrounding the castle's original inhabitants.
ISBN 0-7868-0286-3
[1. Fairy tales.] I. Jermann, David, ill. II. Title.
PZ8.B6415Se 1997
[Fic]—dc21 96-46838

The Secret of the Lost Kingdom

MICHAEL BOLTON

Illustrated by David Jermann

Hyperion Books for Children
New York

The tour bus slowly wound its way around the steep mountain road. Michael stared out the window in awe as the gray towers of the castle appeared through a whisper of silver fog.

"Jennifer," he said, "there it is." But Jennifer's eyes were already riveted on the breathtaking castle.

"The Lost Kingdom," she whispered. The rest of Mrs. McCracken's fifth-grade class was too busy shouting and singing to notice the castle at all.

"Now remember, class," Mrs. McCracken's voice strained to be heard above the din. "The history of this castle, and the people who once inhabited it, remains a mystery to this day. Our only clues to the past lie in its vast treasury of paintings. Now, as you enter the castle, no pushing or shoving . . ." Her words were drowned out by the noises of the students jumping off the bus and rushing toward the massive gates of the castle.

"Stay behind," Michael said, tugging on Jennifer's arm. He and Jennifer had been on plenty of field trips before, and neither of them liked paying attention to the tour guides. Jennifer smiled mischievously at Michael, and they slipped off into an adjoining room as their class proceeded to the Great Hall.

"Check it out!" Michael stopped before the imposing gallery of paintings framed in gold and guarded by velvet ropes.

"They're so . . . real-looking," whispered Jennifer. She walked slowly in front of the enormous portraits. "He looks like a prince, and maybe that beautiful woman is a princess, don't you think—"

"I am glad you like the portraits."

Jennifer and Michael whirled around to face a tall, distinguished-looking old man.

"Who are you?" Michael asked nervously.

"I am the keeper of the castle," the man replied. Then he turned to Jennifer. "You are very perceptive, young lady. So how is it that you and this young man have managed to lose yourselves from your classmates?"

"W-we were just about to join them," Jennifer said.

"A good idea, but you'll never learn from your teacher what I can tell you about Mentoria."

"Mentoria?" Michael had never heard of the place.

"Yes, Mentoria," the old man repeated. He spoke just above a whisper, and yet his voice filled the room.

"There was a time when Mentoria was one of the wealthiest

and most powerful kingdoms in the land," the man began. "Its fields were fertile, and the king and queen reigned with careful consciences and wise hearts. And into this kingdom was born a son. . . ."

As Michael and Jennifer stared at the painting of the prince, the old man's story seemed to come to life. . . .

"You lose again, I'm afraid, Donnus." Prince Marlon laughed as he jumped from his steed to pull his childhood friend from the mud into which he'd fallen.

"I challenge you to another match right now, and I will surely best you." Donnus's face flushed as he heard himself utter the impossible words. Prince Marlon was not only the most able young horseman in Mentoria, but he was also the most skilled at jousting, archery, and swordsmanship. At the prince's easy smile, Donnus had to grin and forget his embarrassment.

"Your Highness," called a voice from behind them. Both men turned to see a general of the Mentorian army approaching on horseback. "I'm afraid I have bad news. The peasants to the south have still refused to give us access to the great mines, and have also refused to surrender. There are only a few hundred men, but they are determined and fierce, and they are nearly upon us. We have no choice but to fight."

Prince Marlon sighed deeply, looking out into the forest. "But they will be defenseless against our army. It will be a massacre."

"Mordal has made the king's wishes very clear. These peasants have defied the king's orders. They must be . . . put down," the general explained.

"Mordal," Prince Marlon muttered. The high priest was the king's chief advisor, but the prince had never trusted this power-hungry, unscrupulous man.

At that moment a scout on horseback galloped up to them. "The men are awaiting the order to charge, sir," he said to the general.

The general looked at Prince Marlon expectantly. With a heavy heart, the prince nodded.

"Let us begin, then," said the general.

The prince mounted his horse and rode at the head of his army, charging the defiant and brave peasants. He drew his sword and joined in the combat with swift force and cunning skill. The sight and sound of so many wounded and dying young men filled the prince's soul with quiet despair, even as he battled on.

Out of the corner of his eye, the prince glimpsed a warrior who possessed fighting skills unparalleled by any other soldier on the battlefield, save himself. After having defeated a good

number of the prince's best soldiers, the warrior suddenly turned upon the prince, his sword drawn.

"Who are you?" Prince Marlon asked, his hand tightening around his own sword. But there was no more time to speak as the young peasant's sword plunged through the air, nearly piercing the prince's shoulder. The prince drew back, then attacked, and the air sang with the clang and hiss of their swords.

"We are too well matched!" the prince finally cried out after a long hour of battling.

"A truce!" agreed the mysterious warrior. Exhausted, they pulled off their helmets. "I wouldn't wish to kill one whose skills I so greatly respect."

"If your people would grant the king access to the mines, there would be no need for this war," the prince said.

"We are fighting to protect the property and rights of our people," answered the warrior. "But now that we have met, perhaps together you and I can seek to end this–" His words were cut short as a Mentorian soldier suddenly struck him with a crushing blow to the back of his head.

"No!" the prince shouted. He jumped from his horse to where the warrior had fallen, but it was too late.

"You and I could have been . . . friends," the warrior whispered. As he exhaled his last breath, his hands folded over a bronze medallion that hung around his neck.

"Friends," the prince repeated, staring at the soldier's lifeless body.

"Welcome home." The old king smiled as he set eyes on his older son. The victorious army had arrived at the castle gates only moments before, to much fanfare and celebration. But Prince Marlon's face was troubled, and he barely responded to the congratulations that greeted him on all sides. His father noticed immediately. "You seem troubled, my son. What is wrong?"

The prince told him of the mysterious warrior, who was so like himself, and of the many others who fought courageously for what they felt was rightfully theirs. "Father, I've always believed that when I fight for Mentoria, I fight for what is right and just. But if we are going to strip people of their lands and slaughter poorly armed men, then I must leave."

"You are the prince and heir, my son," the king replied. "But you are young, and don't yet understand complex matters of state."

"Yes," Mordal said as he stepped into the room, his robes swirling about him. "It seems the prince does not have the stomach for the realities of politics."

"When the realities of politics mean having the blood of innocent men on one's hands," the prince retorted, "I want none of it."

"Go if you must, Marlon," the king said wearily, raising his hand in a halfhearted blessing. "I know you'll be back."

Early the next morning, he watched his son ride off with only a sword and a sack containing a few possessions. The king whispered softly, "You'll be back, my son."

"Perhaps it is for the best."

The king turned from the window at the sound of Mordal's voice.

"What do you mean?" he asked.

"You forget your younger son, Gillian. Perhaps *he* is meant to be the true heir to the throne."

"Gillian is a fine boy, and a gifted artist and poet. But he has never concerned himself with politics."

"True." Mordal's eyes glittered. "And yet I do not think

you should dismiss him so lightly." The high priest knew that Gillian could be easily deceived and manipulated. Then Mordal himself would rule supreme.

But the king merely shook his head sadly. "I hope Marlon finds what he is looking for and returns home, where he belongs," he said.

Prince Marlon traveled for many months, wandering through the countryside of Mentoria. To the villagers, he was known simply as Marlon, and yet his quiet elegance and impeccable manners never failed to arouse their curiosity about where this handsome young man came from.

One night, while dining at a pub, the prince noticed some ruffians shoving and insulting another man.

"Enough!" the prince shouted, swiftly drawing his sword and neatly slashing every button off one ruffian's shirt. "Perhaps you bullies need to learn some respect." They all gaped at him for a moment, then tripped over each other as they ran out of the pub.

"My thanks to you, good sir!" The man clasped the prince's hand in both of his own. "And now that you've helped me, perhaps I can do you a thoughtful turn as well. My name is Gug, and I would be honored if you would come to my home and share

supper with me and my daughter, Nicole. She has been downhearted lately, and your company would do her a world of good."

The prince agreed, and the two men departed from the pub, toward Gug's modest farmhouse.

"Father, you have brought us a visitor," said the beautiful young woman who stood in the doorway. "Welcome to our home," she greeted the prince shyly.

"I am Marlon," said the prince. The woman's uncommon beauty held his gaze. But something else about her struck a chord deep inside him—her quiet strength and inner peace. He had never met anyone who had affected him this way before.

Throughout the evening, Marlon and Nicole couldn't take their eyes off each other, and when Gug offered Marlon the chance to rest at his home for a few days, Marlon eagerly accepted.

"I haven't seen my daughter so happy in many months. Stay as long as you wish," Gug told him. "We have a small farm, but there is always plenty to do to keep busy."

In the golden scattering of summer days that followed, Marlon and Nicole worked together on the farm, becoming close enough

that many times Marlon was tempted to reveal his true identity as the prince and ruler of the very land they tilled together. Time and time again the words would rise to his lips and he would bite them back, not wishing to disturb the flow of the carefree hours they spent together.

One day Nicole mentioned her sorrow over the loss of the man she was to marry. She said very little about him, just that he was a good man who had died honorably in battle.

"I am so sorry," Marlon said softly. "I, too, have known the sorrow of loss. My mother passed away when I was a child." He was quiet for a moment. "Nicole, have you ever thought about leading another kind of life?" he asked. "The life of a queen must certainly be different from that of a farmer's daughter."

"No, no," Nicole replied with a laugh. "I don't spend my precious hours wishing I were someone I am not and could never be. Besides, I'll wager that our simple life here is filled with more happiness than the life of any queen."

The prince smiled to himself, realizing that in Nicole he had found greater nobility than in many of the shallow men and women who frequented the lavish Mentorian court.

One morning, Marlon was roused from sleep by the blare

of trumpets. It was a call used for heralding a visit from royalty! He dashed from the cottage and into the embrace of Cyrus, the king's most trusted councilman and family friend, who had arrived with his entourage.

"Prince Marlon!" exclaimed Cyrus happily. "At last we have found you."

"My good old friend!" cried the prince. "Come and meet my new friends."

"Prince Marlon?" Nicole and Gug dipped low in a curtsy and a bow. "I did not realize," Nicole said, her face crimson, "that our kind guest was of royal blood."

"I can't waste words, my liege. You must return home," Cyrus said, his brow furrowed. "Mordal is a deadly poison to the kingdom, taking advantage of your father's weakening health to levy taxes on the peasants. And Arenotus, the kingdom to the north of Mentoria, has been attacking our borders mercilessly."

"My father—he is not well?" The prince turned to Nicole. He hated to leave her.

"You must go, Prince Marlon," she said softly. "For our

kingdom." With that, she fled to her room, but not before the prince saw the glimmer of a tear in her eye.

Later that day, when the prince climbed the stairs to Nicole's room to bid her farewell, a familiar object hanging on her bureau mirror caught his eye. It was the bronze medallion worn by the mysterious warrior, who, the prince realized in shock and sorrow, also must have been Nicole's lost love. She was gazing at it, her expression a mixture of sadness and anger.

"I left my kingdom to make sense of an unjust world," the prince spoke softly as he approached Nicole.

"Unjust for hardworking peasants and villagers," Nicole replied, turning away, "not for royalty."

"I cannot explain everything now, Nicole," the prince said. "I can only promise that someday I will. Until then, I hope you will wait for me. I give you my word that I will not forget you."

Nicole raised her head slowly and looked searchingly into his eyes. After a minute, she whispered, "And I will surely not forget you, my prince."

The prince had been absent from his kingdom for only a year, but as he, Cyrus, and the royal entourage made their way back toward

the heart of Mentoria, his soul ached with sadness as he witnessed the poverty and neglect that pervaded the towns and villages that were supposed to have been protected by his father's rule.

"It's Mordal's doing," Cyrus reflected unhappily. "A plague on Mentoria, he is, and possessed of an eerie ability to twist control into his own hands. Your father has never been the same since you left; he has lost faith. And Mordal has been wielding more power than is his right."

"These villagers are a pestilence," one of the horsemen sneered as he cleared the main street of a village they were passing through. "They clutter the streets and prey on the mercy of hardworking people."

"The villagers are hungry and desperate." The prince's jaw clenched in anger. "All my people need is opportunity."

When they stopped at an old inn for the night, Prince Marlon noticed a merchant shouting at a dirt-streaked, ragged boy.

"What has the boy done?" Prince Marlon asked.

"He's a little thief!" the merchant said. "He snatched a loaf of bread from me."

"Please," the boy begged. "I'm just—hungry."

The prince looked at the boy's thin limbs and hollow cheeks, and he was reminded of the many other hungry, neglected children he had seen in his travels through the kingdom. He turned to the merchant and tossed him a coin. "This should pay for the bread."

The merchant closed his fist around the coin and hurried away. The boy stared at the prince. "Thank you, sir! But—who are you?"

"I am your prince, and my companions and I are traveling to the castle to save our once great kingdom. And what is your name?"

"I am Leeham, Your Highness." The boy bowed deeply, then looked up, his eyes shining with sudden hope. "Oh please, won't you let me come with you? I can be of use, I assure you!"

The prince grinned. "Well, Leeham, you are invited to join us, but you must promise me your absolute loyalty."

"It is the one thing that is mine to give, Your Highness." Leeham replied. "I will prove myself worthy."

"The king is not much longer for this world," Mordal whispered to himself, adjusting his mink collar in the mirror. His wavy reflection grinned back in a flash of yellowed teeth. "I'll sign the new tax in his name today, and reap the rewards."

"A word with you, if I may, good priest." The shadow of

Cyrus fell across the doorway. "I am here to deliver the kingdom's lost treasure. I present to you—Prince Marlon."

Mordal's stiff smile could barely conceal his shock and dismay, even as he bowed before the prince and welcomed him.

"And this is my squire, Leeham." The prince smiled fondly as he presented the boy.

"I have heard much about you," Leeham said, looking evenly into the priest's pale eyes. His candid stare momentarily broke Mordal's confidence.

"He is quite insolent for a child so young," Mordal remarked with a sneer.

"Leeham is entrusted into my care. And if anything should happen to him . . ." The prince suddenly pulled an apple from his sleeve, tossed it into the air, drew his sword, and sliced it into four even pieces that plopped at Mordal's feet. "The offender will be drawn and quartered with as much speed."

"Welcome, Prince," Mordal said. "But are you certain that returning to the castle, to the center of power and political . . . realities, was a wise decision? Many things have changed here. You may find it rather dangerous to remain for long."

"Empty threats will not turn me away from the kingdom I

have come home to protect," the prince replied. "I assure you that I am quite capable of dealing swiftly with danger."

The king looked fragile as he slept in his canopied bed, the quilts drawn to his chin. His breathing was labored and uneven.

"Father."

The king's eyes squinted to focus on the shape before him.

"Marlon," he whispered, half-rising from his cushions. His hands reached out to his son. "It means so much to me to see your face again."

"Our country is being destroyed, Father," the prince said, kneeling at his father's bedside. "What has happened here?"

"I was blind," the king muttered, pressing his fingers to his eyes. "Mordal used my trust to steal my power. Now I fear I am too weak and ill to be of use."

"Mentoria will be great again." The prince stood, drawing himself up to his full height. "I give you my word." And even as he spoke, the prince felt the burden of his promise, and he remembered the other promise he had made, to Nicole. He shook her image from his head. That time will come, he thought.

⁘ ⁘ ⁘

In the meantime, the chaos throughout Mentoria was echoed in the halls of the High Council. The day after arriving at the castle, Prince Marlon and Leeham disguised themselves to observe the council. They watched in disgust as the politicians waged their battles of selfish pride, without any thought to the suffering people of the kingdom.

In whispers, Marlon and Leeham discussed a plan of action. Then Marlon took the podium and revealed his identity to the High Council.

"For far too long you have let your self-interest rule your debates, accomplishing nothing. You have contributed to the ruin of Mentoria," the prince announced to the gasps and murmurs of the politicians. "Now you shall spend your time more wisely. For the next week, none of you will leave this building until emergency measures have been taken to aid the citizens of the kingdom."

The hall was silent. Prince Marlon strode out of the room, leaving Leeham to moderate the proceedings, and assigning royal guards to make sure every politician remained to do his duty to the people.

But Mentoria was still under attack. The armies of Arenotus, taking advantage of its weakened state, had been waging small,

bloody battles for many months, laying claim to lands that stretched across the outer regions of Mentoria.

"We have two choices," Cyrus said grimly to the prince as they looked out over the castle walls. "Either we gradually relinquish Mentoria in the name of peace, or we call our country to arms and prepare to fight for all that we have."

"And for all that we have lost already," the prince added. He grew quiet, thinking about the unnecessary bloodshed of war, the wasted human lives—especially that of the brave soldier whose bronze medallion was, for the prince, a constant reminder of the need for peace. "But it is so difficult for me to make this choice, Cyrus. For me to sign a decree of war is also to sign a death warrant for so many of my people."

"But Marlon," Cyrus placed a hand on the prince's shoulder, "what is the alternative? To allow your kingdom to be overtaken by the Arenotians? I beg you to reconsider."

Prince Marlon did not sleep for days. He haunted the garden and castle corridors like a ghost. He studied the paintings of his ancestors in the Great Hall, taking comfort in their grave faces. He took his meals privately in his room, but more often than not, the servants cleared away his dishes untouched.

"He will become sick," the attendants whispered among themselves. "And then we will have no leader at all."

The black mood that had settled over the castle grew even more dense when the old king died quietly in his sleep. As the prince watched the great funeral procession wind its way through the village, he realized what he had to do.

"My people are loyal to their king and kingdom," he thought. "And so I, too, must be loyal in preserving their right to freedom."

That afternoon, the prince ordered the entire Mentorian army assembled.

"Our time has come," he shouted. "No war is ever won without a full commitment to vanquish the enemy!" But even as his people cheered, Prince Marlon's heart was heavy. The army was much smaller than he had thought. They would be unevenly matched against the Arenotians. Still, he led his forces out to the battlefield.

There the prince saw a horrifying sight. The army of Arenotus was terrible in its endless ranks. The Arenotian general raised his arm and the trumpets blared their battle cry.

"Prince Marlon, look!" One of his commanders pointed

to the south. The prince turned. Descending from the hilltops in numbers too vast to count, Mentorian farmers and villagers, led by Gug, swarmed to take their places at the battle lines.

"My friends!" the prince exclaimed.

"Your citizens!" shouted Gug. And the battle began.

The prince drew his sword and charged. He seemed to possess superhuman strength. Again and again his sword clashed against the enemy's; again and again he felled Arenotian soldiers.

The prince dismissed the blows that grazed his body until his vision became blurred and his hands slipped from the reins of his horse. Then the world went black.

"Marlon. My prince. Please, wake up."

The prince's eyelids fluttered and then his eyes focused, staring up into the face of an angel. No, it was not an angel, he realized; it was . . . "Nicole! What are you—?"

"*Ssshh,* save your strength," Nicole smiled. "You were badly wounded, but we were victorious! Mentoria has defeated Arenotus."

"This is a great day," said the prince as he sank back against a pillow. "My father would be proud." He suddenly remembered the bronze medallion and struggled to sit up again. "I must explain—the medallion, your—"

Nicole put her finger to his lips. "Cyrus has told me everything. Don't worry."

"Not quite everything," said Cyrus, who, upon seeing that the prince was awake, now joined him at his bedside. "I wanted to tell you myself of Mordal's terrible treason. Half the army never joined you, because Mordal ordered them, in your name, to remain behind and guard the castle. If it were not for Gug and the good citizens of Mentoria, all might have been lost. And for that you have Leeham to thank." Shyly, Leeham stepped forward into the doorway. Cyrus continued, "He overheard Mordal's plot, and he rode alone day and night to reach Gug and to ask him and his countrymen for help."

The boy bowed low. "I promised you my absolute loyalty, Your Highness."

The prince smiled. "You have earned my trust, Leeham, and a place in my court."

"One more thing, Marlon." Cyrus unfolded a letter that he held in his hand. "Mordal is no more a high priest than I am. This letter is from the elders of the church, disavowing any knowledge of him."

"Arrest Mordal immediately," the prince declared. "And exile him to a place where he can do no damage to anyone but himself."

⁘ ⁘ ⁘

Three months later, the new king and queen of Mentoria stood on the balcony, waving at the cheering people. Gillian, Cyrus, and Leeham, smiling broadly, stood at their sides.

"A beautiful wedding," murmured Cyrus. "And a special day for all."

The king raised his hand to silence the people, and when he spoke, his voice was strong and true with the belief in his words.

"I hereby decree, from now until the end of time, that it is the birthright of every man and woman in Mentoria to live with hope and honor and dignity."

"Long live King Marlon and Queen Nicole!" shouted the people.

"And they did live for many years, and so did their children, and their children's children," finished the old man. "Now you have my story. Tell it to the others, and tell it well."

"We will," Michael and Jennifer said in unison.

The old man smiled, turned on his heel, and was gone.

⁘ ⁘ ⁘

"But that's impossible," sputtered Mrs. McCracken. "No one knows what happened to these people. Mentoria! Prince Marlon! Who gave you all this information?"

"The keeper of the castle," said Michael.

"Ridiculous," said the teacher.

"Maybe he was just a crazy old man making things up," said Jennifer as they climbed onto the bus and settled into their seats.

"Maybe," Michael said. As the bus drove away he felt a strange weight in his pocket. He pulled it out. There, on his palm, was the bronze medallion.

"Jennifer, look!" he exclaimed.

Jennifer's mouth gaped open as they stared back at the castle. From the highest tower, the old man was waving. Suddenly, they realized who the knowledgeable keeper of the castle was.

Michael whispered in astonishment, "Cyrus."